ROMANCE, ROMANCE
and
THE BRIDE

ROMANCE, ROMANCE
and
THE BRIDE

FARRUKH DHONDY

faber and faber
LONDON · BOSTON

First published in 1985
by Faber and Faber Limited
3 Queen Square London WC1N 3AU

Set and printed in Great Britain by
Redwood Burn Ltd, Trowbridge, Wiltshire
All rights reserved

© Farrukh Dhondy, 1985

British Library Cataloguing in Publication Data

Dhondy, Farrukh
Romance, romance; and The bride.
I. Title
822   PR9499.3.D5/

ISBN 0-571-13548-X

ROMANCE, ROMANCE

CHARACTERS

PATEL
CHADDHA
BUNNY SINGH (aged about 30)
PREM (aged 21)
SAIRA (aged 21)
SATINDER (SATI) (aged 21)
IAN
LYLA (aged 19)
MR JONES
MRS CHADDHA
MRS PATEL
ANNOUNCER
GITA PATEL
BHANGRA DANCERS
KATHAK DANCERS
QUWALI SINGERS
AUDIENCE, USHERS, etc.

Romance, Romance was first transmitted on BBC2 on 9 December 1983. The cast included:

PATEL	Jagdish Kumar
CHADDHA	Saeed Jaffrey
BUNNY SINGH	Derrick Branche
PREM	Commer Akhtar
SAIRA	Rani Singh
SATINDER	Rita Wolf
IAN	Dale Bayford
LYLA	Dadina Sagger
MRS CHADDHA	Charubala Chokshi
MRS PATEL	Meena Biharie
ANNOUNCER	Ishaq Bux
Producer	Peter Ansorge
Director	Jon Amiel
Designer	Nigel Jones

1. INT. SWIMMING POOL. LATE AFTERNOON
A swimming pool in a private club somewhere in suburban Birmingham. Two middle-aged Asian men, rather unwieldy in body and not very aesthetic, labour earnestly at the breast-stroke. They swim up to the ledge of the pool and take a rest. One waits for the other. They are CHADDHA *and* PATEL. *They are out of breath.*

PATEL: Tones up the whole body, Chaddha sahib, keep going, keep going.

CHADDHA: No, sir. Enough. I should pop into the office before the assistants knock off.
(*As he says this we see a spruce young Asian man,* BUNNY SINGH, *amble up the side of the pool in a very business-like manner and in rather playboyish swimming trunks. He dives in and while they watch does a very fast two lengths.*)

PATEL: Ah, Bunny Singh. Well done, sir. Showing the old men how it's done, eh?

BUNNY: (*From the other end of the pool*) I used to be able to show the young men a trick or two.
(BUNNY *begins another length.* CHADDHA *and* PATEL *begin to get out of the pool.*)

CHADDHA: What style . . .
(CHADDHA *and* PATEL *pull themselves out of the pool. They reveal very middle-aged swimming trunks sodden with water.* BUNNY *starts another vigorous swim.*)

BUNNY: (*Pausing in his swim*) Had enough, have you?

CHADDHA: Oh yes, Bunny sahib. I'm afraid duty calls.

BUNNY: Never say no to a man who pleads business. See you later.
(BUNNY *gives them a hearty wave and begins to swim vigorously. They watch and turn away. As they walk to the changing rooms we take in the sights of the club: plastic chairs, exercise machines, etc.*)

PATEL: Very smart blighter. Three months in town and he's already taken over the Conservative Association.

CHADDHA: Really?

PATEL: Idea and enterprise wallah. Who else but Bunny Singh (*chuckles*) picks up frogs' legs in South India, flogs them in Paris? Eight hundred per cent mark-up.

CHADDHA: Wah! Wonderful. One to watch!

PATEL: Every Indian mother would be proud of such a son-in-law.

CHADDHA: Or every Indian father?

PATEL: What?

CHADDHA: This Bunny Singh of yours. He'll be looking for a quality family, won't he? How is that daughter of yours ... Sita?

PATEL: Gita.

CHADDHA: Oh yes, Gita. She's a very steady girl, isn't she?

PATEL: Very steady.

CHADDHA: I wish my Satinder was. This university business...

PATEL: Your Satinder ... wonderful girl. Accomplishments galore. She must be mixing pretty freely, eh?

CHADDHA: Now, now, Patel sahib, we don't speak of our daughters like that any more.

PATEL: But Chaddhaji, I tell you sincerely, they're still a worry: education, dowry, trousseau. (*He pronounces it 'troosyo'.*)

CHADDHA: Trousseau!

PATEL: Coming for a drink afterwards?

CHADDHA: No, sir, mammoth and myriad tasks await me ... gala ... office ...

PATEL: Achha!

CHADDHA: If you're not doing anything, why don't you and the missis join us? Little dinner party. Intimate, small thing.

PATEL: Oh, thank you, very kind.

CHADDHA: Good. Round eight?

PATEL: Informal?

CHADDHA: Oh, totally, just us, wife and Satinder, and I've called Bunny Singh.

2. INT. UNIVERSITY DRAMA STUDIO. LATE AFTERNOON

A group of drama students are rehearsing a play. They include
SATINDER CHADDHA. *She has written the play and directs it.*
There is PREM, *a young man in the same year as* SATINDER, *doing*
his finals. There are also LYLA *and* SAIRA. *A young white man,*
IAN, *is stage managing.*

A row of chairs marks where the audience is supposed to be. In the
centre sits SATINDER. PREM *and* SAIRA *are on the stage area.*

The scene they are rehearsing is between a young Asian man and
his sister. PREM *plays the man and* SAIRA *the sister.* LYLA *has a*
pillow tucked under her Salwar to denote pregnancy. In the scene
they are discussing their parents.

PREM: (*In character*) You know what they say, that the sins of
    the fathers catch up with their sons . . . and . . . and their
    daughters.

SAIRA: (*In character*) That's the Hindu idea of Karma. It's a
    tyranny. It's a cop-out. We have to take responsibility for
    what we do. Our actions are our own.

PREM: (*In character*) But the past does catch up with us. We are
    prisoners of its customs, its prejudices. I know Daddy is
    wrong, but he's not completely to blame . . .

SAIRA: (*In character*) Even you've started making excuses for
    him . . .

    (SATINDER *claps.*)

SATINDER: No, Saira. Hold on, that's wrong.

IAN: (*Prompting*) 'You don't know what he suffered . . .'

SATINDER: No, hold on, Ian. That was very good, Lyla.

SAIRA: Me?

SATINDER: Yes, I saw it as a little softer, you know, because we
    don't ever see Dad but we build up a picture.

PREM: Every time I say the lines about him I have a picture of
    my own dad. He had all these fierce obsessions, you know.
    (SATINDER *can see that he is about to start one of his stories*
    and cuts him off. LYLA *removes pillow and sighs.*)

SATINDER: Yeah, great. Listen, Prem, when you say, 'Daddy's
    not completely to blame . . .'

PREM: Of course, he's innocent.

SATINDER: No. He's trapped. One side Indian tradition – simplicity, purity. On the other side he's trying to climb the British ladder – the mortgage, the video, the Toyota, you know.

SAIRA: Only too well.

SATINDER: Well, show it, love.

SAIRA: 'Love'? I wouldn't take that from a male director.

IAN: I don't think she meant it like that, Saira.

SAIRA: Oh yes, she did.

PREM: There we go. Started again. 'Love', the most misunderstood word in the English language.

LYLA: Shall I put my cushions back?

SATINDER: Yes, please. Let's take it from the top again.

IAN: 'You know what they say, that the sins of the fathers . . .'

PREM: You know what they say, that the sins of the fathers catch up with the sons and the daughters.

SAIRA: Hang on, please, Sati. Who am I? I don't know where I'm coming from, you haven't given me any blocking, and I don't understand my motivation.

SATINDER: I think an Asian audience would understand, and I think we should just try and get through the scene.

PREM: Excuse me, Satinder is right. They understand love. (*Starts imitating an Indian Movie. Holds his heart with both hands and protests love to* SATINDER, *singing*:) 'Kabhi, Kabhi . . .'

SATINDER: (*As Hindi film character, flutters eyelids and turns away, playing hard to get, then joins in song. Snapping out of it*) See? These Hindi film clichés destroy our youth. Shall we go back to scene one?

3. EXT. CHADDHA'S HOUSE. EARLY EVENING

SATINDER *is walking down the road towards the house.* MR JONES *is washing his car.*

SATINDER: Hello, Mr Jones.

MR JONES: Hello, Sati.

4. INT. HALL OF CHADDHA'S HOUSE. EARLY EVENING
*Continuation. A suburban semi in a pretty middle-class district of
Birmingham.* SATINDER *comes into the hall in which there is a hat
stand with umbrellas and coats. She picks up a letter addressed to
her. It has already been opened.*

SATINDER: Mum, who opened this letter?
> (*She pulls it out and reads it.* MRS CHADDHA *comes in and
> stands, a bit embarrassed.*)
> Where is he?

MRS CHADDHA: You didn't tell us you were applying for this job.

SATINDER: Where is he?

MRS CHADDHA: In the study.
> (SATINDER *walks off to the study.*)

5. INT. CHADDHA'S STUDY. EARLY EVENING
Continuation. CHADDHA *is sitting at a table with a stack of mail
next to him. He smokes a pipe. There are trophies in the room and
photos of* SATINDER *as a little girl in a dress with a huge bow. She
slaps the letter down on the desk.*

CHADDHA: Oh, Satinder. I'm sorry, opened it by mistake. So
much mail coming through on this gala . . .

SATINDER: That was a private letter addressed to me.

CHADDHA: Private? My little girl can't keep secrets. She comes
out in goose-pimples, doesn't she, when there's something
on her mind? (*Turns in his chair.*) Now, missy, I thought
you promised us you were going to finish the teaching
course, so what's this about the Sheffield Crucible?

SATINDER: Everybody was applying, so . . .

CHADDHA: So, write to them very politely and say your daddy is
a monster and won't allow you any freedom to ruin yourself.

SATINDER: Ruin myself. You're so corny sometimes.

CHADDHA: If my sister had said that to her father, oh Baap rey!
She would have been locked up on bread and warm water.

SATINDER: So what's new? Only the menu has changed.

CHADDHA: Just be a sensible girl which we know you are and
. . . (*Returns to a pile of correspondence and poster.*) Do you
want to help the ogre with his organization? Or do you

13

want to help Mummy with a pudding?'

SATINDER: You really are too much. You opened my letter!

CHADDHA: Satinder, darling, it's all right, I understand. You told us you were never going to apply for acting jobs. I caught you at it, eh? Now you feel guilty.

SATINDER: Me?

CHADDHA: Yes, that's all right. Don't worry, I understand. Prodigal son wanders and comes back.

SATINDER: Daddy, darling, you don't have a son. And you're in for a little shock, you know. One day I won't come back.

CHADDHA: All right. Tomorrow. Day after. But tonight, why don't you for once volunteer to help your nasty daddy with his chores?

SATINDER: Lick a few stamps, do your typing, make the tea.

CHADDHA: Why not? All these feministic things. How old are they? Three years? Six years? Indian culture, my dear, is six thousand years old.

SATINDER: It looks it.

CHADDHA: So what about Indira Gandhi?

SATINDER: You know, Daddy, you're a con person. I'm actually very annoyed with you.

CHADDHA: It happens. (*Goes back to his papers.*) Next year the gala will be in the Albert Hall, London. Twenty thousand people.

SATINDER: On an Asian nostalgia trip.

CHADDHA: Your play you are doing. How many people will come? Huh? Eight multi-cultural wallahs and ten educated Indians who already know what you're trying to put across.

SATINDER: It's useless trying to put anything across to you.

CHADDHA: Did Mummy tell you about dinner tonight? There's someone we want you to meet. Come presentable. No jeans!

SATINDER: No harm in wanting. I've got rehearsals.

CHADDHA: Please.

(CHADDHA looks appealingly at her.)

SATINDER: I'll see.

CHADDHA: No, you won't see, missy. You're under orders.

6. INT. THE CHADDHA HOME. EVENING

A dinner party is in progress. There's CHADDHA *and* MRS
CHADDHA, PATEL *and* MRS PATEL *and* BUNNY SINGH. *A place
has been laid for Satinder but she is not in evidence. The dining
room has wallpaper, an impressive-looking sideboard, expensive
furniture in the down-market Harrods style (certainly not Heal's or
Habitat). There are Indian statuettes all round the room, brass,
stone, carved wood. A light is directed on to these statuettes. There is
an embarrassed lull in the conversation.*

BUNNY: (*About the statuettes*) That Nataraj, Mrs Chaddha,
South Indian?

MRS CHADDHA: From Delhi, Government Emporium.

BUNNY: (*To* CHADDHA *and* PATEL) They now ship them off to
Australia and America – roaring market for Indian antiques
out there. I've dabbled in it a bit. Khajuraho, very popular
over there.

MRS PATEL: Very fine things.

MRS CHADDHA: (*Pointing*) That's Satinder's favourite one, that
one, the handmaiden.

CHADDHA: The tenth-century handmaiden. (BUNNY *taps the
video appraisingly.*) Grundig 2000. My dear Bunny, come, a
little topper-upper for you. BB, you're going too slow ...
and some for Daddy.

BUNNY: When am I going to meet the enchanting Miss
Chaddha?

CHADDHA: (*To* MRS CHADDHA) Where is she? I had asked her
to be here.

PATEL: I don't ask. I tell my daughter what to do. Girls today
need a firm hand. Bunnyji.

CHADDHA: She overstretches herself. University work,
community work. (*To* MRS CHADDHA) And you never insist
with her, do you?

MRS CHADDHA: She said she'll be back in half an hour.

MRS PATEL: These girls, no time sense.

CHADDHA: My dear Bunny, I hear you've been invited to edit
the new Asian magazine.

BUNNY: Ah yes, the magazine. We should have had one ten years ago. The mistake our community makes is to imagine they can get something out of the Labour Party. Who passed the first discriminatory laws?

CHADDHA: Quite, quite. The reason why our people go that way is because they are mostly peasants.

PATEL: Those people, they give us such a bad name. They spit here, there, everywhere.

MRS PATEL: So shameless!

BUNNY: They start going wrong when you give them too many toys – videos, washing machines, hire purchase.

MRS CHADDHA: You are for older traditions, right, Mr Singh?

BUNNY: Yes, very much so.

MRS CHADDHA: Although there are some customs . . .

BUNNY: For instance, Mrs Chaddha, I could never marry an English girl.

CHADDHA: Of course not. The community expects something of its leaders.

BUNNY: Ah, not only the leaders. (*Pause.*) There are times when the supporters have to come up with the goods.
(*Some embarrassment follows as* CHADDHA *takes this as a dig about him not having produced his daughter.*)

CHADDHA: Yes . . .
(CHADDHA *motions to* MRS CHADDHA *to bring in the next course.*)

MRS CHADDA: I'll bring in the biryani and korma.

CHADDHA: And some bhindi for Mrs Patel.

MRS CHADDHA: Yes, of course.

CHADDHA: Now let's move on to the fleuri moureau fontaine.
(*He offers round the wine.*)

7. EXT. THE CHADDHA HOME. NIGHT
After the dinner party. CHADDHA *and* MRS CHADDHA *say goodnight to their guests.*

PATEL: Coming to the club tomorrow?

CHADDHA: I probably will.

PATEL: Bunny! Beautiful BMW, yar!

CHADDHA: Sssssh! Well, bye-bye. (*Goes to* BUNNY.) Now, my
dear Bunny, what can I say?

BUNNY: Nothing. It's been a really interesting evening. I'm
glad I came.

CHADDHA: Well, I'll send you the information about the gala.
(BUNNY *reverses out of the driveway.* CHADDHA *storms past*
MRS CHADDHA *into the house.*)

8. INT. HALLWAY. NIGHT

Continuation. We see CHADDHA *putting on his coat.*

CHADDHA: She's not that busy with her drama. It's just plain
bloody defiance.
(*He storms out of the house with the keys to the car in his
hand.*)

9. INT. UNIVERSITY DRAMA STUDIO. NIGHT

*The lights and furniture are now arranged. The production is
becoming more organized.* SATINDER, PREM *and* SAIRA *are
on stage.* SATINDER *wears her normal Western clothes but has
a drape round her head to signify an 'orrhni'.*

PREM: (*In character*) I know Daddy's wrong, but he's not
completely to blame.

SAIRA: (*In character*) Even you've started making excuses for
him now, honestly!

SATINDER: (*In character*) You don't know what he suffered. He
was so hurt, Anjali, when you told him he licks the boots of
the bosses.
(CHADDHA *comes in and stands, wearing his long dark coat
and carrying car keys in his hand at the door.* SATINDER *sees
him, pauses and then resolves to carry on.*)
(*In character*) In our village back at home we were poor.
The landlords in the village were powerful men. They had
the right of life and death over us ordinary people. We
came to Britain with one suitcase in our hands and a lot of
hope in our hearts. Your father wasn't a fool. He didn't
think the streets of London were paved with gold, but he
believed that you could walk down them with your head

held high whether you were white or black or brown.
Britain was a promise which turned into a hard bargain.
Your father would say, 'One day there'll be enough to save,
to go back home.' And as the years passed he knew
tomorrow would come if he lived through the day and the
long long night. But you children, you've never
understood . . .

IAN: (*Prompting*) 'But you children, you've never understood
the sacrifices we've had to make . . .'

SATINDER: Hi, Dad.

10. INT. CHADDHA'S CAR. NIGHT

The scene starts in the middle of an argument.

CHADDHA: Spying? Who was spying? I have a right to know
what you are up to.

SATINDER: You have no right to show me up in front of my
friends. All over some stupid bloody dinner with one of
your fat greasy business cronies.

CHADDHA: You haven't even seen him. You don't know Bunny
Singh! If you saw him . . .

SATINDER: 'Bunny Singh' – ridiculous! Why doesn't he call
himself 'Donald Duck Singh'? No wonder people laugh at
Indians.

CHADDHA: Just watch your step, missy. You think you know
everything. Just because you go to college. Who pays? Who
pays the fees?

SATINDER: My bloody grant, if you must know.

CHADDHA: And put your seat belt on! It's all my mistake, for
treating you like an equal. I thought: all right, she'll settle
down, get serious about things . . .

SATINDER: I am serious. At least I think about it . . .

CHADDHA: You write one silly play and you think you know
everything. What do you know about India? You've never
even been there.

SATINDER: More than you do. Your pathetic health
club and stupid annual gala for the peasants . . . You
think they don't know you're patronizing them?

Oh God, you make me laugh!

CHADDHA: You'll be laughing on the other side of your face soon.

II. EXT. THE CHADDHA HOME. NIGHT

CHADDHA *brings the car to a halt in the driveway and* SATINDER *slams the door after her.*

SATINDER: Bullshit!

12. INT. HEALTH CLUB EXERCISE ROOM. DAY

CHADDHA *and* BUNNY *are working out on an exercise machine.* CHADDHA *is flagging.*

BUNNY: Take it to the limit one more time, Chaddha sahib.

CHADDHA: My dear Bunny, I'm at my limit. People let me down all over the place.

BUNNY: Family problems?

CHADDHA: Stubborn, headstrong girl. You know.

BUNNY: She sounds like my sister. Out of all of us she was the worst. In her college days she was full of Naxalite stuff and communism. Lovely girl.

CHADDHA: What happened to her?

BUNNY: We got her married. Husband, two cars, chauffeurs, children, responsibility – complete transformation.

CHADDHA: Complete bloody transformation.

BUNNY: Complete.

CHADDHA: So, my dear Bunny, you approve of a bit of rebellious fibre?

BUNNY: Best material to work with. The cowboy movies are right . . .

CHADDHA: Cowboy movies?

BUNNY: Yes. Tame a wild stallion and it makes the best mount. (CHADDHA *stares and then laughs uncertainly.*)

CHADDHA: Makes the best mount! I say, Bunny, why don't you be our guest of honour at the gala?

BUNNY: I'd be delighted.

CHADDHA: And after we'll have a little drink, eh? Make it a family occasion.

BUNNY: Always at your service, Chaddha sahib.
(CHADDHA *applies himself to the machine with gusto.*)

13. INT. CHADDHA'S STUDY. NIGHT
CHADDHA *is perusing the poster for his gala variety performance.*
He hears the door slam outside.
SATINDER: (*Out of vision*) Bye, Mum.
(CHADDHA *disappears for a second and comes back with*
SATINDER.)
CHADDHA: Just two minutes, missy.
(SATINDER *follows him into the study. He shows her the*
poster. It has a group of Indian classical dancers on it. It reads:
'Gala Cultural Evening sponsored by the Asian Arts and
Cultural Association'.)
CHADDHA: Like it?
SATINDER: Very nice.
CHADDHA: The Asian Arts and Cultural Association strikes
    again. Do you want one for the University?
SATINDER: I'll pin one up if you like.
CHADDHA: Satinder darling, how long is your play?
SATINDER: About fifty minutes.
CHADDHA: Hmm. Bit longish.
SATINDER: For what?
CHADDHA: Well, I thought you young people might like to use
    about twenty-five minutes in the gala. A drama spot.
SATINDER: To do our play?
CHADDHA: Why not? I think I can persuade the committee.
SATINDER: Twenty-five minutes.
CHADDHA: Yes, you see, we need some balance. Something to
    make them think. All the rest is song, music, dance. Has
    your play got a good story?
SATINDER: I don't know, can't say. I wrote it. I suppose we
    could cut it down. Yes. Daddy, this is fantastic. Thank
    you.
    (*She gives him a big baby kiss.*)
CHADDHA: So Daddyji is not such a bloody fuddy-duddy after
    all. And Satinder, no swearing, eh?

SATINDER: Course not.

CHADDHA: I understand. But keep the volume button low on the politics.

SATINDER: It's all about understanding, Daddy. The younger generation discovering what's right about their roots.

CHADDHA: Fine, fine, written, directed and starring Miss Satinder Chaddha.

SATINDER: It's a co-operative, Daddy.

CHADDHA: Fine, fine, fine.

14. INT. UNIVERSITY DRAMA STUDIO. NIGHT

The actors are sitting in the stalls of the theatre, stunned by SATINDER's *news.*

SAIRA: Half an hour?

SATINDER: We cut out the sub-plot. Just concentrate on the Britain scenes and leave out the village ones. I've worked it all out.

SAIRA: Hang on, what about my funeral pyre scene?

PREM: Good. I couldn't get the Indian accent anyway.

SAIRA: My speech in that scene was central to the whole concept of women's liberation. You only had three lines in the whole thing.

IAN: Can I say something? If we lose the Asian scenes, we'll lose the sense of ... of ... kind of ... (*Searches for the word.*)

LYLA: Humour?

IAN: ... alienation.

SATINDER: Look, we've got a real audience. They'll be coming in coach loads. It'll be fantastic. Prem, you know where you shout, 'The bastards, the bastards'? Don't. Say something else.

PREM: 'The illegitimates, the illegitimates'?

SATINDER: No, say, 'The swine.'

SAIRA: Well, the Muslims won't like that.

SATINDER: What then?

PREM: 'The silly cows.'

LYLA: The Hindus won't like that.

SATINDER: Stick to 'bastards'.

21

15. INT. CHADDHA'S BEDROOM. AFTERNOON

It is the day of the gala. CHADDHA's *and* MRS CHADDHA's *twin beds are separated by a bedside table with a reading lamp on it. There are books there: Harold Robbins, some* Woman's Own *magazines, a Punjabi newspaper. The cupboards and wardrobes are open and* SATINDER *sits on the bed looking through a suitcase full of her mother's old clothes.* MRS CHADDHA *is standing on a chair and taking from the top of the wardrobe a little-used bundle of festive sarees. These are wrapped up in a muslin cloth to keep them from dust and give them a special place.*

SATINDER: Mum?

MRS CHADDHA: Yes.

SATINDER: Haven't you got anything black or just plain white?

MRS CHADDHA: Like funeral sarees?

SATINDER: No, like working-class or Punjabi peasants wear.

MRS CHADDHA: Tch, of course I don't have any such things.
   (*Gets bundle on bed and unwraps it.*) Why don't you wear old Salwar Khamiz, they always wear such things. And drape over head?
   (SATINDER *finds a Salwar Khamiz which is plain and baggy She holds it up. It's a very plain, baggy Khamiz.*)

SATINDER: Mummy! What's this?

MRS CHADDHA: Oh that! That's something your aunt left. I can't throw it out.
   (SATINDER *pulls out of a special bundle of clothes a very skimpy dress with narrow straps, a nylon affair that would necessitate baring the shoulders and is the sort of dress that a show girl would wear.*)

SATINDER: Mum, what's this?

MRS CHADDHA: Oh, that's not mine, stupid thing . . . from long ago, before you were born. I've kept it.

SATINDER: What for?

MRS CHADDHA: Your father used to work for this (*giggles*) . . . his first job as accountant. They had a fancy-dress party. All-English firm. In London I was working and I asked an English friend and we went out and bought this.

SATINDER: He took you out, wearing this?

MRS CHADDHA: (*Remembering her youthful gesture of independence*) I thought, everybody's wearing something daring, why can't I? I just turned up. He couldn't say anything.

SATINDER: You should wear it again.

MRS CHADDHA: Don't be silly. I'm much too old and fat now. (*Looks at saree.*) Why don't you wear this one for afterwards?

SATINDER: Afterwards?

MRS CHADDHA: With Daddy's guests. All the young girls will be wearing sarees. You should look the prettiest when he introduces you to Bunny Singh.

SATINDER: (*Looking at her mother and sussing something*) Mummy, not you too?

MRS CHADDHA: So many young girls are being shown to Bunny, you know. B. B. Patel has high hopes. He's a very good catch. Highly educated.

SATINDER: So. I'm on display, am I?

16. INT. DRESSING ROOM AT THE GALA. EARLY EVENING
Some Bhangra dancers are messing around, singing and cracking jokes. PREM, *putting on his make-up and beard, jokes with them.* SATINDER *enters. Shouts and jokes from the boys.*

SATINDER: Everything's changed. I want an urgent word with all of you. Prem, this could be your big night.

17. INT. HALL FOYER. EARLY EVENING
Two spruced-up MEN *greet* BUNNY *as he is ushered in by* CHADDHA *and* PATEL. *People are standing around before the event showing themselves off.* PATEL *clicks his fingers to attract the attention of his* DAUGHTER *who comes up from a group of girls whom she is with to be presented to* BUNNY SINGH. *He extends his hand to shake hers. She, when introduced does a 'namastey', hands joined as though in prayer, as a greeting.* BUNNY *put his hand away and she, realizing the gaffe, extends hers. They all laugh.*

18. INT. HALL. EARLY EVENING

The hall is filling up. YOUNG MEN *walk about with pseudo-importance.* CHADDHA *ushers* BUNNY *to the guest-of-honour seat in the front.*

BUNNY: Chaddha, it's nice to see a community occasion starting on the dot.

19. INT. DRESSING ROOM. EARLY EVENING

The girls are applying make-up. SATINDER *puts on a long-haired black wig.*

SATINDER: Mmm, Rita Hayworth. What do you think?

LYLA: It's lovely.

20. INT. HALL. EARLY EVENING

CHADDHA: We start with a bang. Bhangra. These boys from Derby, superb I tell you. Sense of rhythm and costume, I went out there specially to get them.

BUNNY: A very impressive gathering, Chaddha sahib.

PATEL: Half of them come for the show, half of them come to see you.

(CHADDHA *looks around. His eye is shifting constantly to see if the arrangements are going well. The sound system comes on.*)

ANNOUNCER: Testing, testing.

CHADDHA: They are always testing. They should be ready. These boys ... Bunny, excuse me, I'll just see to it.

ANNOUNCER: Not testing any more.

(*The crowd laughs.*)

CHADDHA: Have to leave you and address the masses, heh, heh. B. B. will look after you. *Arey B. B. Bunny sahab ke liye Kooch Coca Cola vugera ...*

PATEL: Yes, yes.

(CHADDHA *goes.*)

21. INT. STAGE AND HALL. EVENING

The lights dip. We see CHADDHA *at a microphone. Camera turns to* MRS CHADDHA *and* BUNNY *sitting next to each other.* PATEL *brings drinks and slips down in the chair next to the guest of honour.*

The stage curtain is drawn.

CHADDHA: (*To audience*) Ladies and gentlemen, I have the very pleasant task of welcoming you to the Third Annual Gala of the Asian Arts and Cultural Association. I'm afraid I'm going to bore you between items by appearing. I hope you all know me. I am, of course, your humble secretary, Pradip Singh Chaddha.

(*Hoots and cheers.*)

Second in the squash men's final this year, but unbeaten in golf.

(*Hoots and cheers.*)

We are very pleased to have with us today Mr Bunny Singh, who is the new editor of the Anglo-Asian Conservative Association magazine and who has won the Chamber of Commerce Award for the most enterprising business man of the year and brought some glory to our community. Mr Bunny Singh!

(BUNNY *stands up and turns to the crowd with a 'namastey' and they clap.*)

But I'm sure the artistes we have assembled today, the best that the Midlands can offer, are here for your entertainment and I'm certain you will enjoy yourselves. So without much ado about nothing, we present to you, ladies and gentlemen, the first item on the programme, an ensemble of Kathak dance. You will observe that two of their dancers are new to the troupe, but really in the spirit of multi-racialism.

22. INT. DRESSING ROOM. EVENING
PREM *removes his beard and begins to apply film-star make-up.*

23. INT. HALL. EVENING
The KATHAK DANCERS *are in full swing. Two of the troupe of dancers are white, in the spirit of multi-racialism.*

24. INT. HALL. EVENING
CHADDHA *is up on stage again doing his MC bit. The stage curtain*

is closed.

CHADDHA: And now, ladies and gentlemen, something rather special. A short drama written and directed by a Ms Satinder Chaddha who will also be appearing in it along with her friends from Birmingham University. And – how can I put it? – I am proud to confess that Ms Chaddha happens to be my daughter.

(*Applause.* CHADDHA *steps off the stage. He goes and sits by* BUNNY. *The curtain opens to disclose* SATINDER *in the skimpy dress without a blouse that she has taken from her mother's room.* PREM *and the others, also dressed in garish, improvised outfits, are in support. We see* CHADDHA's *face: dismay and puzzlement.* BUNNY *shifts in his seat but doesn't look at* CHADDHA. *The drums strike up and* SATINDER *goes into a Runa Lalila song.*)

BUNNY: You've included this sort of filmy *ganna* too?

CHADDHA: It's . . . must be part of their play . . . I can't understand this. What is she doing?

(*The song now changes to a duet.* PREM *comes forward and gives a serenade Hindi film style.* SATINDER *stands on stage, her hips thrust out, looking alluring and fluttering her eyelids rapidly in a very stagey manner. The* YOUTHS *at the back of the audience show their approval by clapping and whistling.* CHADDHA *stands up to see who is clapping and whistling.*)

Who are these churlish fellows?

(SATINDER *and* PREM *never touch on stage but they make dance gestures in Hindi film style which are suggestive of the soppy romance that is the stock in trade of the Indian movie. The other girls meanwhile are in the chorus and do a regular Western pop chorus girl act.*)

BUNNY: And that's Miss Chaddha?

(CHADDHA *and* MRS CHADDHA *are well choked.*)

CHADDHA: We didn't commission this. She's not like this. That's enough, they are making a mistake . . .

MRS CHADDHA: (*In Punjabi*) I can't watch this any more. I'm going.

(*She gets up and* CHADDHA *follows her.*)
CHADDHA: Arrey, darling, wait.
(BUNNY *frowns. The song goes on.*)

25. INT. STAGE AND WINGS. EVENING
CHADDHA *stands in the wings and he motions to* SATINDER, *trying to catch her eye. He is distressed, and attempting to be persuasive rather than angry.*
CHADDHA: Satinder, darling, what are you doing? This is not the play. Satinder!
(*She catches his eye and she turns back to the stage. The song is in full swing and she swings it.*
CHADDHA *fumbles around the wings and finds the curtain cords and brings the curtains together. There is a roar of disappointment and some appreciation from the crowd.*)

26. INT. HALL. EVENING
Immediately afterwards the curtain comes up again and we see the QUWALI SINGERS *setting themselves on stage. They begin. The leader gives a small chant in Urdu. During this we see* BUNNY *saying something to* MR PATEL. *Then he goes out, bending low so as not to intrude between audience and show.*

27. INT. GREEN ROOM. EVENING
BUNNY *sits on the sofa, just a flicker of amusement on his face.* PREM, LYLA, IAN, SAIRA *all come in laughing.* SATINDER *follows them, more pensive. Her trick has had repercussions she didn't exactly bargain for. She has to pass* BUNNY. *He rises.*
BUNNY: Miss Chaddha. We meet at last. I'm Bunny Singh.

28. INT. CLUB BAR. EVENING
Moments later. One or two people are buying drinks. CHADDHA *sits at the end of the bar, crestfallen.*
SATINDER *comes in and spots him. She hesitates, then plucks up courage to approach him. He looks around.*
CHADDHA: Your mother's gone home. In tears.
SATINDER: Yes. Now, can we talk?

CHADDHA: Talk? We didn't deserve this from you.

SATINDER: All right. Maybe it was a bit over the top?

CHADDHA: You don't think of your mother, you don't think of me, you don't think of my position . . .

SATINDER: I thought I was supposed to be thinking of your Bunny Singh.

(CHADDHA *registers some surprise. It is the first he has heard of her discovery of his little scheme.*)

I was on show. How do you expect a showgirl to behave? I was . . .

CHADDHA: (*Raising a hand*) Enough, enough. What kind of impression do you . . .

SATINDER: He got a very good impression. I was talking to him. He even made me a proposal.

CHADDHA: What!

SATINDER: He's offered me a part in one of his movie deals. Discover a new starlet from UK.

CHADDHA: Bunny said that?

SATINDER: He's smart. He knows what's what. Who's good to marry and who's good to put under tight contract.

CHADDHA: Darling Satinder, I was sincerely trying to give your play a chance.

SATINDER: Come on, Daddy, not quite sincerely. You wanted to . . .

CHADDHA: All right, all right. (*Changes tone; curious*) What kind of contract was the fellow offering you? You're not interested in that sort of acting . . . are you?

SATINDER: Well, you didn't want me to go into acting, did you?

CHADDHA: Well, I don't know. It would be something to think about, but would you be happy?

SATINDER: Well, I don't know. It'd be something to think about.

(*We see a small but explorative reconciliation.*)

THE BRIDE

CHARACTERS

TONY (aged 22–3)
TEACHER
JASWINDER
JUNAID
DEBBIE
CHARLIE
CAR SALESMAN
LADY
YOUNG GIRL
JASWINDER'S NEIGHBOUR
JASWINDER'S FATHER
PUPILS AT SCHOOL

The Bride was first transmitted on BBC2 on 11 November 1983. The cast included:

TONY	Phil Daniels
TEACHER	Michael Carter
JASWINDER	Janet Steel
JUNAID	Andreas Ramlingum
DEBBIE	Debbie Roza
CHARLIE	Roy Heather
CAR SALESMAN	Anthony Trent
YOUNG GIRL	Satwant Bhambra
JASWINDER'S NEIGHBOUR	Rashid Karapiet
PUPILS AT SCHOOL	Prabal Chatterjee
	Lydia Ferguson
	Angela Ramlingam
	Parvinderpal Sains

Producer	Peter Ansorge
Director	Franco Rosso
Designer	Ian Ashurst

1. EXT. SCHOOL PLAYGROUND. AFTERNOON

TONY, *a young White man, stands outside the school gate. He looks up at the buildings. He looks down the street. He is dressed in tatty jeans, an old shirt and an army surplus jacket. He lets himself into the school by opening the gate. He goes round the back of the building and tries the door at the back. It lets him in.*

2. INT. SCHOOL CORRIDOR. AFTERNOON

TONY *walks through. He pauses in the corridor at the entrance to the classrooms and the hall. He looks into the deserted hall. We see signs everywhere of the school being on holiday. The chairs are on the desks. The furniture has been moved round. There are tins of floor polish lying in the hall where the caretaker has left them while taking a break.*

TONY: (*Voice over*) It took a bit of bottle but I had to come and find you. No one else would believe it, right? Maybe no one else cares. You used to go on at us about how things get you. They got me. I had to tell someone.

3. INT. CORRIDOR OUTSIDE A CLASSROOM. AFTERNOON

TONY *stands at the door. He looks into the classroom. There is a* TEACHER *there. The* TEACHER *is unloading books from various opened cardboard boxes. He doesn't notice* TONY *who watches him.*

TONY: (*Voice over*) I remembered something you used to say to us. What was it? You don't get rich by working hard. You get rich by making other people work hard.

4. INT. CLASSROOM. AFTERNOON

We see the TEACHER. TONY *is in the doorway. The* TEACHER *has the feeling he is being watched and turns around.*

TEACHER: Well, well, well, look what the wind blew in. Long time no see, Tony! What brings you here?

TONY: Tell you the truth, I come to find you.

TEACHER: How did you know I'd be here in the holidays?

TONY: Saw your car outside.

TEACHER: Didn't run into it, I hope.

TONY: Ain't got mine no more.

TEACHER: Been banned?

TONY: Nah. I gave it away. Shanks's pony and London Transport now. Straight up, I'm not rich any more. Three years old, these Levis. Easy come, easy go. Can I sit down?

TEACHER: Come easy, did it?

TONY: That's what I came to tell you. I gave it away. You had something to do with it.

TEACHER: Me? You gave away all that money.

TONY: It's a funny story, but on my mother's life it's true. I want to tell you about it.

TEACHER: I've got to stash these in the stock cupboards.

TONY: Hang on, I want to . . . like tell you.

TEACHER: I'll be back. (*Picks up cardboard boxes and labours out.*) You stay there. I'll be back.

TONY: Yeah. (*Voice over*) You had me well sussed. See I didn't make the cash . . . I was lying. I didn't thieve it, neither. She gave it to me. Jaswinder. It was her who made me rich.

5. EXT. SCHOOL PLAYGROUND. DAY

The school is in recess and the KIDS *of all ages play in the grounds.* TONY, *in a sleeveless vest with military jeans and a skinhead haircut, strolls along the netting outside. The* KIDS *see him and his appearance excites their attention. They crowd around the fence and begin to jeer. He walks on towards the entrance. We see graffiti behind him on the school building walls:* 'Sikhs rule: top-knot boot boys'; 'Alien culture: punjab jabbers'.

TONY: (*Voice over*) I was brought up to think White. My dad's a racialist. When I was a kid he used to go on about it. What do you expect? I grew up with them Pakis. What else can a poor boy down here do?

(*The other* BOYS *with* JUNAID *in their midst come and grab his Doc Martins.* TONY *dodges them, tries to step on their hands, and they pull him off the wall by his ankles. He jumps to avoid*

34

crashing down. The BOYS *are on him. They playfully touch his head. A dozen hands go to his new haircut. They say, 'Skinhead', 'Whoo', Texture boy'. They get hold of him and put him on the ground. He struggles a bit. But not as though he is serious. They put him down and spread his arms and nail them as though crucifying him. We see* JUNAID *step with one foot on* TONY's *chest. The* LADS *move off him. He raises himself on his elbows. They run off so as not to be caught by him and as the group disperses he gets up.*)

TONY: (*Voice over*) I knew you used to think I was right prejudiced, but it warn't that. I don't think you teachers knew what was going on down there. We was in the minority, right? And it was our country, but you wouldn't allow us to say it.
(*He dusts himself off.* JASWINDER *and her friends approach him.*)

JASWINDER: Tony, what the hell have you done to yourself?
(TONY *pretends to examine his elbows for scars and cuts.*)

TONY: (*Voice over*) I fancied her something rotten, even in the juniors, but I never let on because it would have shown me up in front of me mates.

6. EXT. SHOPPING ARCADE. DAY

A crowded Saturday. An Indian café's exterior. We can see TONY *sitting at a table and looking out through the plate-glass front. He stares down the street, waiting. From one end of the pavement come* JASWINDER *and her* DAD. *The* DAD *is a Sikh man of imposing height and stature. He wears a turban and has a very striking moustache and beard.* TONY *steps to the doorway of the café as they pass.*

TONY: (*Voice over*) I knew that on Saturdays she'd go shopping with her mum on the Broadway, so I used to hang about the café, and wait for her, and check her on her way down. And she'd be so shy or cautious or whatever, and hardly say hello when she was with her mum and give you a total blank if she was with her dad. I carried a picture of her tattooed on my brain.

(*We see* JASWINDER *passing without acknowledging* TONY's *presence.*)

7. INT. NEEDLEWORK CLASSROOM. DAY
Tapestries hung on the walls. Crochet-work, smocking, etc. A class full of Asian girls. They cluster around JUNAID. TONY *sits on his own.*

TONY: (*Voice over*) Sure, I made a fool of myself. I used to hang about her like a thirsty dog and they knew, they all knew, she musta known. In the sixth form I even chose everything she'd chosen – subjects, I mean, geography, home economics, and needlework.
(*We see* TONY *earnestly trying to thread a needle.*)
(*Voice over*) The only geezer she had eyes for was Junaid. The girls, they'd wet their pillows for him if not their knickers. 'Ah, poor fellow, poor Junaid.' See, he was an orphan, brought up in care – Dr Barnardo's was invented for him. On my life he lived on it. And he was your favourite, wasn't he?
(*We see* TONY *still trying to thread the needle. He pokes himself and bleeds. Nobody looks at him when he says 'Ahhh.'*)
All right, Tone, you'll have to suck it yourself.
(*He puts his thumb in his mouth.*)

8. INT. DISCO. NIGHT
The fifth-year room is decked out for the disco. It is shadily lit. A DJ *plays records and has a light show going. The* TEACHERS *and* PUPILS *dance together. Couples are getting intimate in the dark corners. The* TEACHER *and a* BOY *are lounging about at the door. The disco plays a lovers' rock tune.* TONY, *looking somewhat gaunt and anxious, turns up at the door. He stands silhouetted against the light and the* TEACHER *spots him.* TONY *looks, trying to adjust his eyes to the darkness of the further corners of the room.*

TEACHER: Oi, Tony, ticket!

TONY: Ain't got one.

TEACHER: I announced it at three fifth-year assemblies. All tickets to be paid for the day before. No fares at the door!

TONY: I was skint . . . yesterday.

TEACHER: So? Your credit's good with me.

TONY: Yeah, and get shamed up in front of the class.

TEACHER: How we supposed to pay Jimmy Saville and the sounds?

TONY: Ain't you goin' let me in, then?

TEACHER: No. Say please.

TONY: No. I know why you won't let me in, cos I'm white.

TEACHER: Don't be so feeble.

TONY: It's true. Everybody knows that you're on their side.

TEACHER: Go on, get in.

TONY: It's all wog music anyway. (*Voice over*) When I finally plucked up courage at the end of the fifth year and asked her whether she was going to the school disco, she replied that her dad was too strict. But she made it in the end. (TONY *strolls into the darkness towards the record player. He sees* JUNAID *kissing* JASWINDER *in a corner.* TONY *rips the record off the turntable with a quick motion and flings it away.*) (*Loudly*) Lights out at the orphanage at eight. Homeless mongrels should pack it in, and go back to their slum. (*The* DJ *turns one of the house lights on. Everything comes to a standstill and* JUNAID *comes for* TONY *who hits him in the face. There are a few screams and* TEACHERS *and* JASWINDER *rush to separate* TONY *and* JUNAID. *The* TEACHERS *get hold of* TONY *and frogmarch him out. He tries to retain his dignity.*)

TEACHER: You're a bloody idiot.

TONY: Good! I'm glad.

TEACHER: Why did you do it?

TONY: She lied to me.

TEACHER: Who?

TONY: Jaz. She was gonna come with me.

TEACHER: She didn't come with anybody.

TONY: How come he always wins everything, eh?

TEACHER: Who?

TONY: Junaid, you sucker.

TEACHER: Just wash your mouth out and get out.

(*The* TEACHER *pushes* TONY *into the playground.*)

9. EXT. SCHOOL PLAYGROUND. NIGHT.

A few moments later. TONY *has paused to gather his wits and to
cool down. He looks to see if he has been pursued.* JASWINDER
comes up out of the darkness.

JASWINDER: What did you do that for, Tony? You're not like
that.

TONY: You know why?

JASWINDER: You're like a brother to me.

TONY: Some brother, I know you don't like me.

JASWINDER: Yes, I do. I'm not . . .

TONY: Then how come you turn up and when I ask you, you
said you wasn't coming.

JASWINDER: I wasn't going to come. I didn't lie to you. You
don't understand. I had to sneak out. You know what my
dad's like. I don't know what he's going to do to me when I
get home!

TONY: (*Voice over*) I tell you what I did then.
(*We see* TONY *grabbing her.* JASWINDER *grapples with*
TONY, *pushes him away and runs back to the building.* TONY
watches her go.)

10. EXT. STREETS. NIGHT

TONY *comes out of the school gate. He is bouncing with the
immediate memory of the stolen kiss.*

TONY: (*Voice over*) I went home with my head singing. It was
worth it. And as I walked home by the yellow sulphur
light, I was that dopey with that kiss. I thought 'Romeo,
Romeo – where art thou?' or whatever it was. Pure
Shakespeare. Straight up, have you ever loved somebody, I
mean fancied her, that it made you sick?

11. INT. CLASSROOM. MORNING

Before school has started. JASWINDER *and a group of* GIRLS *are
looking at a manuscript. A handwritten thick thing.* TONY *comes in.
One or two* GIRLS *seem to be finishing their homework in a hurry.*

Some BOYS *lounge about waiting for the bell.*

TONY: What's that? (*He goes to take it and* JASWINDER *pushes him away.*)

FIRST GIRL: Junaid's homework. His autobiography. 'My Life of Sorrow'. Done yours?

TONY: Yeah, seventeen lines. The short happy life of Anthony Bathurst Esquire. How many lines Junaid got?

JASWINDER: Fifteen sides and it's good. Maybe you ought to read it. You might understand how lonely he is.
(JASWINDER *gives him the manuscript.* TONY *starts reading it and turns away from the group of* GIRLS.)

TONY: Yes, I'll go and have a look.

12. INT. CLASSROOM. MORNING

The class is in session. A GIRL *is collecting the homework and hands it to the* TEACHER. TONY *comes into the classroom and sits down.*

TEACHER: (*Going through the homework*) What is this? 'The Short Happy Life of Anthony Bathurst Esquire'. DO it again.

JASWINDER: That's my homework and that's Junaid's, sir.

TEACHER: Junaid's? You trying to write the sequel to *War and Peace*?

GIRL IN CLASS: Yeah, read it loud sir. It's fantastic.

TEACHER: Right, Junaid's then. Do you mind if I read your your work to the class, Junaid?

JUNAID: If you like.

TONY: Read the second chapter, sir.

TEACHER: All right, all right. (*Looking through*) Then, when I was eleven, the council advertised for foster parents. I remember looking at the ad in the home. It had my picture and it said Junaid would be grateful for a home and all that stuff. And then some people did apply and the workers looked through the applications and they were nice so they even asked me which ones I preferred. I said, 'Why didn't they send their flippin' photographs, you sent them mine', but I only got dirty looks. Anyway I was sent off to a family who had a house in London and a farm in Wales. They

were quite posh. That was my second foster home and it
lasted only three months. (*Turns page.*) You see on this
farm there was pigs and that's where my sex life began.
(*The class is astonished.*
So is the TEACHER, *but he doesn't want to stop reading and*
adopts a poker face.)
They was fat and pink and hairy and I was so
frustrated . . .
(*The* TEACHER *trails off. He frowns as he reads the next*
sentences. The BOYS *all laugh. The* GIRLS *don't quite know*
how to react and are silent.)
Junaid?
(JUNAID *gets up and grabs the folder out of the* TEACHER's
hand, tears it up. He flings the paper and storms out. The
PUPILS *laugh.*)
Junaid!
(JASWINDER *runs after him.*)

13. INT. CLASSROOM. DAY
JASWINDER *is reading a letter.*
TONY: (*Voice over*) Dear Jaswinder, You think I'm an animal,
   right? I swear I changed Junaid's story for a laugh. I didn't
   realize he'd take it so hard.
DEBBIE: Watcha, Jaz. What you doing there? Love letters from
   Junaid?
JASWINDER: It's from Tony. Says he's sorry. What do you
   think I should do about him?
DEBBIE: (*Reading letter*) 'It's hard for me to say what I really
   feel about you, but please don't hate me. It would hurt me.'
   Hurt him.

14. EXT. PLAYGROUND. DAY
It is class time and the SENIORS *are playing football, supervised by*
the TEACHER (*of the framing story*) *in a track suit. The* BOYS *are*
playing five a side. JUNAID *and* TONY *are in short shorts, as are the*
rest of them. They wear school football shirts.
The BOYS *troop out of the gym as* JASWINDER *and her friends come*

down the stairs. TONY *passes them and* DEBBIE *stops him.*

TONY: I thought you weren't talking to me.

DEBBIE: Jaswinder wants a word with you. Put your arm out.
(JASWINDER *ties the rakhi on his wrist and kisses him on the cheek.*)

TONY: What's this in aid of?

DEBBIE: It's an Indian custom.

TONY: What's it mean?

DEBBIE: You got to give her a present first before she can tell you. Anything, it doesn't matter what.

TONY: I've got something.
(TONY *takes a gold sovereign off his neck and puts it round* JASWINDER's *neck.*)

JASWINDER: It means you're my brother now and you've sworn to protect me. Like a brother. I really like you, Tony, but not in that way, you understand.
(*The* GIRLS *go back upstairs.* TONY *walks away down the corridor.*)

15. INT. CORRIDOR. DAY

We see JUNAID *pausing in the corridor. He overhears the conversation and then moves on to the hall window from which he can see some transaction. He straightens up and moves down the corridor to the washroom.*

TONY *follows him down the corridor wearing the rakhi. He looks at it.*

16. INT. WASHROOM. DAY

JUNAID *is at the wash-basin.* TONY *comes into the room and starts at the other wash-basin next to him. There are other boys around changing from shorts back into school uniform. Piles of gear. Clothes lie around the room.*

JUNAID: You hot? What's that? New skin charm?
(TONY *looks at the bracelet as though he's just remembered it.*)

TONY: You could say that.

JUNAID: Where did you get it from?

ANOTHER LAD: Jaswinder.

JUNAID: What is it? What's it mean?

(TONY *kisses the bracelet.*)

TONY: What's an engagement ring mean?

(TONY *looks up defiantly at* JUNAID. JUNAID *thrusts his hands through the toilet window and cuts himself at the wrists. He looks at his wrists melodramatically as they bleed.* JUNAID *collapses on the floor and the* BOYS *gather at the sight of blood. One of them rushes out to fetch the* TEACHER. *The* TEACHER *rushes into the changing room and pushes the kids off, away from the unconscious* JUNAID.)

TEACHER: What's he done this time? Call the Head, tell him to get an ambulance.

(TONY *is there, hanging about. A little serious, chastened, as he watches the drama going on around him.*)

TONY: (*Voice over*) They went to get you and you took him up the hospital. She had to follow him up there, didn't she? And her dad came and dragged her away and threatened Junaid for messing with his daughter. Right Indian film stuff . . .

17. EXT. STREET MARKET. DAY

TONY *is standing next to a barrow that sells briefcases and artificial leather luggage. Next to him is a barrow that flogs electronic stuff. He has two or three packing cases piled on top of each other. The noise of the market gives way to his voice.*

TONY: (*Voice over, as he unpacks art jewellery from a suitcase and arranges it on a cloth.*) When I left school I got these deadbeat jobs. Thirty, maybe forty sheets a week. Shit. Then my uncle goes to me, Tone, do a bit of sales representation for my firm, will yuh, and I got all this clobber.

18. EXT. STREET MARKET. EVENING

The market is quiet now. A few straggling CUSTOMERS *hurry home. It is a cold winter's night. The lamps of the stalls are not all lit. The market is packing up, vegetables and cardboard boxes strewn everywhere.* TONY *is not at his box.*

TONY: (*Voice over*) I used to trade from off this geezer's barrow. I was well late, I remember, cos it was the day after me birthday and I'd had a few jars with the lads. There was no one else about. The place was deserted.

(*The barrows have been packed up. We see* TONY *coming out of a pub door on the corner carrying his suitcase of jewellery. He goes back to where he trades and begins to look for something (his suitcase strap). He finds it and starts strapping his box up.* TONY *looks down the street and he sees in the mist at a distance of a few yards the outline of a woman standing by a lit barrow.* TONY *approaches her. We see from her reflection in the glass cases on the barrow, which also have costume jewellery in them, that it is* JASWINDER. *She is dressed in a saree and a cape.*)

We're closed. Jaswinder? (*As she turns to show her face*) Stop me dead, what are you doing here?

JASWINDER: Looking. These yours?

TONY: Is that all you've got to say to me?

JASWINDER: I'm in a hurry.

(*We get a close-up of her face and see tears on her cheeks.*)

I was to be married today. It's my wedding night.

TONY: Don't spring that on me.

JASWINDER: My father arranged a marriage with my neighbour's cousin.

TONY: Listen to me. This is bloody England. You don't have to marry this geezer. Your dad can't tell you what to do.

JASWINDER: No. He can't. But I'm to meet my bridegroom and I must have something to wear.

TONY: Didn't your dad get you anything? How did you get here?

JASWINDER: You were here. I tied a bracelet on your wrist three years ago.

TONY: I know and I promised. I'll do anything you want. Just name it and if I can do it, I'll do it.

JASWINDER: It's England and I can't do what I like.

(*She laughs, a small, cynical laugh.* TONY *is puzzled. He frowns.*)

TONY: I've got jewellery. I'm in the trade. (*Unstraps his box.*) Jaswinder, it's just trinkets but you can have them if that's all you want.

JASWINDER: It's all I want. An anklet of gold. A bride should have a gold anklet.

TONY: That's tall. (*Rummages through box.*) I picked up something today. (*Drags out some chains.*) Maybe not perfect, but it's something, real gold.

JASWINDER: You were always a bit gone on me, weren't you, Tony?

(TONY *holds out the chain but she doesn't take it at first.*)

TONY: Not a bit. A lot.

(TONY *fiddles with the chain and makes it into a sort of anklet by fitting a clasp on it. It's three chains with a sort of gold stud on each chain. He kneels down and puts it around her ankle.*)

JASWINDER: I knew you'd help. Thanks, Tony. Goodbye.

(TONY *looks up at her.*)

19. EXT. STREET MARKET. DAY

We see TONY *drinking a cup of tea from a stall elsewhere in the market. Then he turns and comes back to his own box. Trade is slack. People don't pause before either* TONY's *stall or* CHARLIE's. TONY *goes to his box and unpacks it. He is doing it mechanically and picks a piece of jewellery out and then does a double-take. He has in his hand a very elaborate, expensive-looking anklet.*)

TONY: He's doing all right over there.

CHARLIE: Who?

TONY: Reggie, flogging them towels.

CHARLIE: Well, I'm glad he's doing all right. We could be doing all right an' all, if you got that stall set up.

(*The box has other jewellery in it. His own stuff is gone.* TONY *looks at it. Then he looks at* CHARLIE, *who is trading away.*TONY *laughs as though he's sussed the practical joke.*)

TONY:I've been stitched up, Charlie.

CHARLIE: What you talking about? Nice bit of flash, that. Good gear. Shouldn't have trouble flogging a few of those to our dusky cousins, son.

TONY: But it's real, Charlie.

CHARLIE: Eh, what do you mean, real? My God! Where did you get this? No, don't tell me, I don't want to know. Just get it in the case and get it off my stall and into the van. We only have straight stuff in here – no bent gear, understand?

TONY: When I went to get the teas, Charlie, did you see any Indians hanging round here?

CHARLIE: Sure, Tonto came riding by. Now look, for once in your life do what I say and get this stuff off.

TONY: You sure you're not winding me up? My name is Billy, not Silly, you know.

CHARLIE: That's all we need – as advertised on *Police Five*. Now get rid of it.

TONY: You sure no Indians tampered with my box?

CHARLIE: No one touched it, Tone, now get it in the van and lock it.

20. CAR SHOWROOM. DAY

TONY *approaches down the street.*

TONY: Three months later the law tell me the stuff's clean. No reports of it stolen or missing. The money was mine.
(*He pauses and reaches in his pocket for a wad of money. Then we see the bracelet on his right hand.*)

21. CAR SHOWROOM SHED. DAY

American cars are lined up in a meretricious display. TONY *comes out of the office with the* CAR SALESMAN. *They stand in front of the car* TONY *wants to purchase.*

TONY: Three grand.

CAR SALESMAN: Three eighteen.

TONY: Three thousand two. Don't bother to count it, it's all there.

CAR SALESMAN: It had better be all there, Tony, or I'll be round to see your mother. Listen, kid, be careful. This thing moves so fast you are liable to catch pneumonia.

TONY: (*Referring to price tags*) The other one.

CAR SALESMAN: You'll pull the birds so fast, you'll need a transplant.

(TONY *revs and zooms off.*)

22. INT./EXT. CAR/STREETS. DAY

TONY *is driving.*

TONY: (*Voice over*) I knew it was her all the time. It had to be Jaswinder. She's made me rich. I recalled she was marrying a rich geezer, a goldsmith, and every day I thought about it. But how had she got them into my case? I let it play on my mind for a year. Putting an end to a mystery is always scary for me, but I picked up the courage. I drove down to check her house.

23. EXT. STREET. DAY

TONY *knocks at a door. a* LADY *opens door. She is suspicious.*

TONY: Jaswinder? She lives here.

LADY: No English.

(YOUNG GIRL *looks over the fence.*)

YOUNG GIRL: You want Jaswinder? That family's gone. They don't live there no more. My daddy knows where they went.

TONY: Go get your dad then.

(*The* YOUNG GIRL *goes into the house and fetches him.* TONY *follows her. Her father,* JASWINDER'S NEIGHBOUR, *appears.*)

JASWINDER'S NEIGHBOUR: Yes?

TONY: Excuse me, do you know what happened to Jaswinder's family?

JASWINDER'S NEIGHBOUR: Whole family gone. One year ago, gone back to India.

(*He turns to go, closing the door on* TONY.)

TONY: Please. Please, I need some information. I was . . . her husband.

JASWINDER'S NEIGHBOUR: Husband? But she was loving a Muslim boy.

TONY: Junaid? I know all about him. We got married secretly. I was her husband. She left me and I want to get in touch with her again.

JASWINDER'S NEIGHBOUR: Just wait one minute, please.
   (*He leaves* TONY *and goes indoors. He comes back into the hall
   with a newspaper cutting which he hands to* TONY *who begins
   to read it.*)

TONY: Dead!

JASWINDER'S NEIGHBOUR: Sad business. Her father was
   forcing her, very rich man but too old he found for her.
   Father was very broken when she kill herself and the
   Muslim boy with her.

TONY: This is dated the twenty-first of July. My birthday. This
   can't be possible. I saw her ... I saw her on the twenty-
   second.

JASWINDER'S NEIGHBOUR: You went to the funeral?

TONY: Sorry, I didn't mean to lie. I wasn't her husband. I was
   lying to make you tell me about it.

JASWINDER'S NEIGHBOUR: What does it matter? But you
   shouldn't tell me these lies.

TONY: I was only her brother.
   (JASWINDER'S NEIGHBOUR *stares at* TONY *who turns and
   gets into his car.*)

24. INT./EXT. CAR/STREET. DAY

TONY *sits in the seat and thinks. Then he turns the ignition on and
looks at his wrist. The bracelet is gone. He switches the engine off.
He looks from his wrist to the floor of the car. He gets out of the seat,
opens the door and gropes on the floor of the car. He retraces his steps
to the* YOUNG GIRL.

TONY: Where is it? The bracelet.

YOUNG GIRL: I never took it.
   (TONY *looks up and down the path. He is frantic. Then he
   grabs the* YOUNG GIRL *by the arms.*)

TONY: Where is it?
   (*He suddenly realizes that he is being crazy and brutal. He
   releases her.*)
   I'm sorry. Oh God. It's gone.

YOUNG GIRL: I haven't got it. You're mad.

TONY: I'm sorry. Look, take the money.
(*He turns and goes back into the car.*)

25. INT. CAR. DAY
TONY *is searching in the car for his bracelet.*
TONY: (*Voice over*) I'd kept that, the rakhi, she'd gave me at
school. I wore it on my wrist. Always. She'd have left me
that, I thought. But then I hadn't acted like a brother, I'd
blown it . . .

26. INT. CLASSROOM. AFTERNOON
TONY *sits where he was at the beginning of the story.*
The TEACHER *comes back.* TONY *looks at him, gets up, goes to the
door – his decision made.*
TEACHER: Sorry it took so long. OK then, shoot.
TONY: Don't matter.
TEACHER: What do you mean, it doesn't matter?
TONY: It just don't matter.
TEACHER: Tony.
TONY: Look, I'll see you around some time, yeah. (*Voice over*) I
wanted to tell you a story.